STIR IN STILLNESS AND OTHER STORIES

STIR IN STILLNESS AND OTHER STORIES

R. N. SHARMA

ATLANTIC PUBLISHERS AND DISTRIBUTORS

Published by
ATLANTIC PUBLISHERS AND DISTRIBUTORS
B-2, Vishal Enclave, New Delhi-110 027
Phones 5413460, 5429987

Sales Office
4346/4C, Ansari Road, Darya Ganj,
New Delhi-110 002
Phones 3273880, 3285873, 3280451
Fax 91-11-3285873
E-mail gupta.atlantc@axcess.net.in

ISBN 81-7156-711-8

Typeset at
APD Computer Graphics, Delhi

Printed in India at
Mehra Offset Printers, Delhi

CONTENTS

PREFACE

I must confess that I am not a man of letters. It is probably an urge to write that compels me to scribble whatever comes to my mind. This collection of short stories is result of this urge and compulsion only.

However, it was probably a word of encouragement from the late Khawaja Ahmed Abbas that gave me confidence. ''Just go on scribbling what comes to your mind, it will automatically take some shape,'' he had once told me, and I followed this golden rule to create these pieces of fiction.

Another person I owe a debt of gratitude is Mr. Vishwa Nath, Editor of Delhi Patra Prakashan (publishers of 'Alive', 'Woman's Era' and host of other magazines). His critical comments, at times very curt and harsh, on the short stories submitted for publication, helped me a lot in looking into the thematic value of my short stories.

I wanted some literary figure to look into these short stories for 'improving' their language or atleast 'polishing' them, and to write a 'Foreword', if possible. But one or two persons whom I approached expressed their inability to do so. Rather, one of them was harsh with me when he said, ''So you would also like to be counted among those Toms, Dicks and Harrys, who are bringing out books of fiction these days with no literary background to fall back upon.''

Well, I may not even be considered fit to be in the list of these Toms, Dicks and Harrys, leave alone be counted.

Finally, I will be failing in my duty if I do not thank my publishers M/s Atlantic Publishers and Distributors and their Directors Dr. K.R. Gupta and Mr. Manish Gupta for undertaking the publication of this 'Collection' which may prove to be a losing commercial proposition for them.

R.N. SHARMA

IT SO HAPPENED .....

Mahesh paced up and down in the balcony. Occasionally he went in the room but came out running whenever there was a roar of an automobile or an auto-rickshaw. He checked time on his wrist watch. It was already half-past six. Usually Monica was back home from her office by five-thirty or so.

She had called him to say, "I might be reaching home late today. Please collect Munna from his creche and on the way get two packets of milk and onions and potatoes also. I think their stocks are exhausted."

He interrupted her to ask, "What time you would be reaching home ?"

She had ignored his interruption and continued, "Please boil the milk and give Munna his evening feed, and ensure that he takes it. Usually he is in the habit of leaving in between."

He again interrupted her, "But darling I want ......"

"..... Please check his nappy also and if wet change it. Don't forget to remind the maid-servant to be on time tomorrow morning."

And without waiting for him to say anything she had disconnected the line.

He was taken by surprise. He had not prepared himself for this sort of contingency. Never in their five years of married life he cared to know how she was managing the affairs of the house. Even after Munna's birth he didn't try to share her burden. He had left all the household affairs to her care. Whether it was buying knick-knacks of daily use from the bazaar, calling a mechanic to repair an electric gadget or leaving Munna at the creche, she managed it. She on her part ensured that there was no disruption.

For Mahesh everything ran smoothly. He got his bed tea and breakfast on time. He always found his lunch box for office ready. Monica almost worked like a clock, counting on each second, to do the morning chores, before herself getting ready to catch her chartered bus.

Monica never felt much fatigued till she was pregnant. She really went through hell during her pregnancy — hypertension, cramps, loss of appetite, etc. Mahesh's occasional lip sympathy was of no consequence to Monica. He thought all this to be her headache.

Mahesh had felt relieved when her parents told him that she should have first delivery at their place. Monica's mother had accompanied her and stayed with them till arrangements for the maid-servant and creche were made.

The hectic mornings did not bother Monica much. It was the evenings, after the tiresome day in the office, that exhausted her. She expected Mahesh to be of some assistance to her at that hour. His presence itself could be of some consolation to her. But he usually came back very late, not before nine or nine-thirty, in any case. The card and drink sessions in the club kept him busy in the evenings; the habit he had inherited from his bachelorhood days. He had continued with it, despite her protests, mild and strong. "For you the house is only an inn, "she had once told him in somewhat jocularly tone, "where you come only to spend your nights."

Monica's protests and small talks to make Mahesh responsible towards the family and its affairs proved ineffective. He remained indifferent, making matters difficult for Monica with every passing day.

Munna started crying. He had wet his bed. He searched for a bed sheet. "Had Monica been around she would not have allowed this to happen," he mused to himself.

He was not able to lay his hands on a bed sheet. He just refolded the wet one and made effort to put Munna back to sleep.

The maid-servant had finished her work in the kitchen and

was about to go. "Be on time tomorrow morning," Mahesh told her as instructed by monica.

"Tomorrow I might take off, Sahib," she said, and left without giving Mahesh a chance to question her further. Mahesh thought of such like situations which Monica might have to face many a time.

Mahesh again looked at his wrist watch. It was already seven. He had done a quite deal of pacing up and down and baby-sitting. He badly needed a cup of tea. Surprisingly none from the neighbouring flats had come to enquire, though Munna had cried a lot.

The door bell rang. He rushed to open the door. A smiling Monica stood before him. He glanced at his wrist watch. It was already twenty-minutes past seven.

"It so happened Mahesh," she began speaking without giving an opportunity to Mahesh to say anything, "as I was waiting for the bus I met an old college friend. We were meeting after almost a decade and decided to go to the Coffee House to talk things over," and probably to further hammer her point, she added, "It was really an enjoyable evening. Perhaps after years I felt relaxed."

The words "it so happened" got stuck in Mahesh's mind. He had very often used them by way of an explanation whenever Monica questioned him for getting back late to home. Probably he was being reminded by her of his indifference towards the family and all that was connected with it.

His guilty conscience pinpricked him.

"I will get you a cup of tea," he said, "You better go and fresh yourself."

She looked straight at him and smiled. "Don't bother. In any case I have to prepare the dinner," she said.

"No, you are not going to go to the kitchen tonight. We are dining out," he said in a tone that Monica had not heard of all these years.

*** *** ***

NO, NOT AGAIN

Manisha refused to undergo the sex-determination test of the foetus. It was already over six-weeks when she had confided to her husband that she had probably conceived again. Hemant was keen on the test. Infact it was his mother who was prompting and insisting on her son to take Manisha to a doctor for the test.

"And if it is again a girl, then ?" Hemant had posed the question to his mother.

"Then let her go in for abortion," the mother had replied without even batting an eyelid.

Manisha had undergone an abortion about six months ago. That was her second abortion in a matter of about a year and a half. At that time also she had protested and resisted. But ultimately the will of Hemant and his mother had prevailed, and she had reluctantly agreed to.

"It is nothing but murder Hemant," she had told her husband. She had talked about the trauma she had to go through after every abortion. "It is better we should avoid pregnancy rather than indulging in this act of infanticide. I really get upset after this," she had pleaded with him.

But Hemant never committed himself to the idea. Like his mother he too was very keen on having a son after two daughters, though lacked the guts to express himself explicitly. His mother, however, always had the grand-son syndrome in her mind. Whether it was the break-fast time or dinner time, she had only this topic to talk. At times Manisha used to take exception to such talks. "Mummy it is becoming difficult to bring up the children these days. Every addition in the family is at the cost of some comfort or even necessity," she would try to argue. But Hemant never came to her support. His silence rather used to encourage his mother. "It is only you who make hue and cry, Manisha," she would counter-argue, and query, "Have you ever cared for what Hemant thinks about the matter?"

Manisha knew it very well that she would never be able to convince Hemant. Whenever she talked to him she found him evasive. "You see Manisha my mother is somewhat orthodox in such matters," he always said to pacify Manisha." It should be our endeavor to ensure that she should not get disturbed on such petty matters."

"These are not petty matters Hemant," agitated Manisha would tell him, and by way of rebuttal, add, "Moreover they concern us, I mean, you and me. Don't you agree with me?"

Manisha's arguments always found Hemant dumbstruck and in a somewhat uncomfortable situation.

Hemant's mother had been yearning for a grandson right from the day Manisha gave birth to her first daughter. "Had you taken her to Baba's Ashram and asked her to take his *bhasams*, she would have certainly been blessed with a son," she had told Hemant. Manisha had refused to oblige her mother-in-law. "It is all rubbish," she had told Hemant. How can these *bhasams* help in such matters?" Her mother-in-law was agitated, but found herself helpless against vacillating Hemant and stubborn Manisha.

But when Manisha conceived for the second time, both Hemant and his mother had taken complete charge of her. She was almost ordered to do what they had prescribed for her. They were not prepared to listen to her, this time.

She was taken to Baba's Ashram and asked to perform certain *poojas*. Baba has given her some 'specially prepared' powder to be taken in the morning for a week. Her mother-in-law ensured that Manisha religiously observed the instructions of Baba.

Both Hemant and his mother were so sure of Baba's *bhasam*, that they did not feel the need of taking Manisha to a doctor for the sex-determination test. "I am very sure your wife is going to deliver a boy this time. Baba's *bhasam* has worked wonders in many cases," Hemant's mother had assured her son and to prove her point she had many tales to relate which she had heard at Baba's Ashram.

Manisha was only amused about the 'humbug' being created by her husband and mother-in-law. Every time she protested, she was over-ruled. She was fighting only a lonely battle.

The only person in the family who had regard for her feelings was Hemant's elder sister Rohini. She was married and had a four-year old daughter. Hemant's mother had been showing her concern for her daughter also.

"You must have another child now," she had been telling her whenever she visited her mother's house. Rohini always had a stock reply to give. "Mummy we have our own plans. We will have our second child when Mini will be five."

"I wish you should have a son next time," was the next thing which Hemant's mother would invariably tell her daughter. Rohini had again a stock statement to make. "We don't mind even a daughter, Mummy. But for God's sake never ever talk about your Baba and his *bhasams* to Sailesh and his parents. They don't believe in such stupid things and will never allow to pursue such rubbish." Rohini's warning had silenced her mother. She was always wary of talking to her about her second child whenever she came to see her.

Rohini had even warned her mother against too much interference in the marital affairs of Hemant and Manisha. "It is their life Mummy," she had very often advised her mother. "Let them plan it in whatever manner they like." But her mother wanted her writ to run in the house. Hemant was also too willing to subject himself to the dictates of his mother.

As the due date of Manisha's delivery came closer, tension started building-up in the house. But Manisha as usual continued to be calm and composed. At the time of her first delivery also she had no tantrums and never got panicky.

Till the doctor informed Hemant and his mother, who waited outside the delivery room, that "it is a girl", they were all the time hoping that it would be a "boy" this time. They refused to believe, "It cannot be. Baba can't go wrong," exclaimed Hemant's mother and addressing Hemant said, "I am sure Manisha had not followed his instructions properly."

Hemant, who too looked disappointed, however, knew it well that Manisha did whatever she was 'asked' to do. She couldn't be faulted.

Both Hemant and his mother took some time to adjust. The mother just couldn't take kindly to the new child and Manisha. "I think I will die without seeing a grandson," she would complain to all and sundry.

Hemant's second daughter was not even one year old when his mother started telling him to go in for another child. Manisha was totally opposed to the idea. "The third child will be too much a burden on us," she had told Hemant. But like his mother he was also struck by the son-syndrome and had ignored all her pleadings. And when Manisha informed him about her conceiving again, he wanted to be doubly-sure this time through the 'test'.

But Manisha refused point-blank to oblige him. "I am not undergoing any test and I will not go to Baba's Ashram for *poojas* and his *bhasams*," she finally told Hemant and his mother. "Either you both agree with me or I go to my parents' place and come back only after the delivery."

Both the mother and the son were aghast at Manisha's assertion. They knew it for certain that she would not tolerate any of their 'nuisance' this time.

Manisha found a great supporter in Rohini. "I am glad you have asserted yourself," she told her. "Come what may both Sailesh and I will stand by you."

Both Hemant and his mother had resigned themselves to the inevitable. They were no more talking about the 'test' and Baba's *bhasams*.

But they were in for another shock, especially the mother. Rohini had given birth to a daughter, the second one. They were further jolted when they went to see her in the Nursing Home along with Manisha.

"Mummy to avoid further pregnancies I have also undergone an operation at the time of the delivery," a smiling Rohini told her mother. "Both Sailesh and his parents have given their concurrence for it."

"You did the right thing Didi," interjected Manisha. Both Hemant and his mother looked at Manisha. For once the usual pale and gloomy face had the traces of glow on it.

*** *** ***

PUNJAB MAIL

Hardit's flight landed on time at Delhi's airport named after the late Indira Gandhi. He felt elated. On his return to London he would proudly announce to others about Delhi having a new and modern airport.

He was visiting India after a gap of ten years. He had in mind only the stuffy and stinking airport where arrivals and departures used to be irksome and tiresome affairs. Now he found the staff also somewhat courteous and cooperative. Hardit was through the formalities quickly. He carried nothing which could delay his clearance.

Nobody was there to receive him. He did not either expect anybody. Who would have come all the way from his village ?

After the usual haggling, jostling and pushing around by the hordes of auto-drivers, he hired a three-wheeler and came straight to the New Delhi Railway station. He had planned it like that only. He wanted to pay his obeisance at Bangla Sahib and Rakabganj gurudwaras. His wife, Kulwant Kaur, had specifically asked him to offer prayers at these holy places.

Punjab Mail was popular with the passengers who travelled between Ferozepur and Delhi and vice-versa. Punjab and Frontier Mails were two trains which had become synonymous with Punjab, before and after the partition. But Hardit had only known the Punjab Mail. It used to be an ideal train for his occasional visits to Delhi and beyond. It was convenient for both down and up journeys. It was touching Kot Kapura, the changeover station for many mofussil places, including his village Bagapurana, at very convenient hours. The day never got wasted. "So it still leaves at the same hour," he muttered as he left the booking window. He considered himself very lucky that he got the booking for the same evening. The reservation in the air-conditioned two-tier had cost him peanuts in terms of pounds.

Instead of taking a room in a hotel, Hardit preferred to stay in a retiring room at the railway station. It was convenient. A young couple was already there. As Hardit disposed of the coolie, he observed that the lady was whispering something to the man.

"I hope I am not putting you to any inconvenience," Hardit said. Though not much educated, his stay abroad had taught him small courtsies. "In fact there is no other room available," he clarified.

"Doesn't matter," the man was somewhat apologetic. "We had booked it only for the night. We are just waiting for the breakfast."

The gentleman had a fleeting glance at Hardit's luggage — two brand new suit cases, an overflowing handbag and a transistor-cum-tape recorder. The lady gave a piercing look at the two-in-one. Hardit had noticed that even coolie was reluctant to carry it. The authorities had repeatedly warned the public not to touch any attractive and strange objects specially the transistors.

"Are you coming from abroad?" the gentleman asked.

"Yes, please, from London." Hardit felt somewhat relaxed. "You look like 'locals' ", he commented. He had picked up the word in England.

"Oh yes, we are coming from Kanpur and proceeding to Amritsar."

"Amritsar," Hardit repeated and bowed his head in reverence.

"Yes to attend the marriage of his niece," the lady interjected. "But for our presence needed over there in connection with some ceremonies, we would not have..."

"It is not like that *Sardarji*," the gentleman was quick to intervene. "The things are not as bad she presumes to be. Probably because she lost her brother in a terrorist attack she carries this sort of a feeling."

Hardit looked at the lady. Her face carried a feeling of anguish. "I share your grief, *Beti*. But rest assured things would improve."

The breakfast ordered by the couple had come. That gave Hardit time to go in for his bath and change.

Hardit had snacks at way side snack-bar and proceeded to Gurudwara Bangla Sahib. He observed the usual hustle-bustle in the vicinity. The surroundings too looked better. He said his prayers and listened to the *Shabad Kirtan*. His next halt was at Gurudwara Rakabganj. He joined the *langar* there. He was feeling tired and decided to go back to the railway station and relax.

The Punjab Mail was on time. The coolie conducted him to the air-conditioned two-tier coach. He was the first to get in. One by one the passengers started trickling in. It was a mixed crowd.

Hardit settled down and took the first opportunity to talk to the passenger occupying the opposite berth. "I am told that the Punjab Mail is hauled by a diesel engine. It must be pretty fast now."

"Not exactly. Rather till very recently it was no better than a passenger train. But of late it has picked up the speed."

The train started moving. Very soon silence descended in the compartment. Only sounds of snoring and chit-chats in some corners disturbed it.

Hardit could not get sleep. His mind travelled back to the days prior to his escape to England. He remembered how his friends Harpal and Mohan Lal had helped him. He was in particular indebted to Mohan Lal for paying for his passage to London.

Hardit's father had never considered his son of any worth and was happy when Hardit had expressed his desire to leave India; but had refused to render any assistance, financial or otherwise. Hardit was hardly twenty when he had landed at London. He had married the second daughter of his neighbour, another migrant from Punjab. It was a love marriage and a very successful one. Such marriages rarely succeed now. The boys and girls develop friendships, flirt for a while, enter the wedlock, and run to the courts for divorce.

Hardit had two sons and a daughter. The present visit to India was primarily to fix his daughter's marriage with Mohan Lal's son, a computer engineer. On his last visit to India Hardit had talked to Mohan Lal about it. The latter had gladly agreed to the proposal. By offering his daughter Hardit wanted to express his gratitude to Mohan Lal for whatever he did at the time of his departure for England.

Hardit did not care for his two sons, both past their mid-twenties. They could get their brides in England. They had been on and off with so many girls that Hardit had stopped keeping a count. They had been only flirting and were never serious. It was no use managing brides for them. But Hardit's only regret was that both the sons had proved to be good-for-nothing fellows. Despite the opportunities available and provided to them, they could not go for higher studies. Both had gone for menial jobs and acquired all the vices of the western society. Hardit had almost written them off.

Unlike her brothers, Hardit's daughter had graduated and was handsomely earning. Hardit and Kulwant had desired that she should marry Mohan Lal's son. Though modern in outlook, the daughter had agreed for an arranged marriage.

"We are approaching Bathinda," somebody announced. Hardit got up and proceeded towards the door. He very badly needed a cup of tea.

Bathinda station presented a dull look. Not many people were moving around. A lone tea-stall *wala* was doing brisk business.

Hardit observed that most of the people were talking to each other in hushed tones. He was missing the usual vibrancy he used to observe after the arrival of the Punjab Mail.

After Bathinda Punjab Mail stopped almost at very station. The day had dawned when it reached Kot Kapura. There were not many passengers to get down. Hardit looked for Harpal and Mohan Lal. They were expected to receive him. But there was no one. "It is something very strange," he mused to himself. He occupied a bench and waited for them.

No tea-stall had opened as yet. "Sardarji are you waiting for somebody?" asked a signalman, Hardit nodded. "Who would come?" the man added. "The town is under curfew." Hardit looked at the man with wide-opened eyes. Curfews were a thing of the past in England now.

The signalman asked Hardit to move to the retiring room. "You have some rest there and move out only when they relax the curfew. Meanwhile I will arrange some breakfast for you.'' The man looked to be a non-Pubjabi; most probably from eastern India. Hardit appreciated the gesture. He moved to the retiring room. The man brought tea and stuffed *paranthas*.

Around noon when Mohan Lal came, Hardit felt relieved. ''The moment they relaxed the curfew I rushed to receive you,'' Mohan Lal explained making an affort to catch up with his breath. ''We have to rush back and pick up from the police station body of Harpal.''

Mohan Lal's statement stunned Hardit. ''What ? ...'' His voice got choked.

''Yes, Hardit. The militants shot Harpal dead while we were coming to receive you. But for him my son and I too would have been killed. He kept the attackers at bay till we escaped to safety.'' Mohan Lal broke down.

Hardit stood still. Harpal's bullet-ridden body flashed before his eyes. ''So Harpal sacrificed his life for my daughter's sake,'' he picked up the courage to say; but couldn't control himself.

He prayed for the departed soul as tears rolled down his eyes. A shrill engine whistle at a distance sent shivers through his body.

***   ***   ***

BORROWED HONEYMOON

As the taxi took a sharp turn, the chilly winds pierced through Randhir's body. He glanced at his wife. She was fast asleep. But her body stirred as the cool breeze touched her. She had almost slumped in his lap. He put his right arm around her shoulder to give her some warmth; ensuring that the other three passengers did not observe him.

Randhir and his wife were returning to Delhi after their honeymoon trip to Shimla.

Randhir was not prepared for this sort of extravaganza. The suggestion had come from his friends and colleagues. "When are you leaving for your honeymoon?" "Where are you planning to have your honeymoon?" Such questions were asked from him the day he had brought his bride.

"Is it all that necessary?" he had countered questioned.

"Yes it is," he was told.

His wife had expressed no opinion, when he had asked her. Probably she had no idea of the honeymoon. As a matter of fact he was not very sure of himself. He had known many a newly wedded couple who had proceeded on their honeymoon trips the day ceremonies of the marriage were over. They had booked in advance air or rail tickets, and hotel rooms.

Randhir had done nothing of the sort. After making bare necessary arrangements connected with marriage, he was left with no money. He had taken all the loans available in his office and exhausted all his savings. He had refused to accept any dowry or gifts. Even his savings were not substantial. As an UDC, Randhir could not have saved more. He had widowed mother and a college-going sister to support. Excepting a two-room flat his father had left no assets to bank upon. The family pension his mother got was just enough to cover the flat's instalment.

"We will fund your honeymoon," suggested some of his colleagues. "You can clear your debts in due course."

Randhir found himself in a very embarrassing situation. "Honeymoon, and that too on borrowed money," he just couldn't imagine. But before he could take any final decision, tickets for Shimla and travellers cheques worth two thousand rupees were arranged and handed over to Randhir. "No excuses now," he was told. "You both will have to leave for Shimla tonight itself."

Next day evening Randhir and Smita were in Shimla. Leaving Smita at the railway station, Randhir went on a hunt to fix a room in some hotel. As he moved from one hotel to another, he was all the time doing mental calculation about the money he could spare for boarding and lodging, contingency that might arise, and of course, for the return journey.

After quite a deal of running around and haggling, he was able to fix a double-bed room for one hundred and fifty rupees per day. "Thank God, it is off-season these days," the manager had informed him. "During the season we charge two hundred and fifty rupees for the same room." Randhir listened to the manager's sermon without any comment.

"But mind you it includes nothing," he was told. "Breakfast, lunch and dinner are charged separately. But you have an option to go out for your meals."

The room was not very airy and provided no scenic beauty. But having come to know that they were on a honeymoon trip, the attendant had taken extra care in decorating the room.

"Probably the man is trying to entitle himself for some tip," Randir had thought.

Randir had not planned the trip. "Honeymoon trips cannot be adhered to a schedule," he was advised. "Relax, rest and just roam about."

They had relaxed, rested and also roamed around aimlessly; lunching and dining wherever and whenever convenient. Randhir meticulously kept account of the money he was spending. He didn't want to cut a sorry figure while checking out from the hotel.

"Let us go back," Smita told Randhir on the morning of the third day. Randhir was taken by surprise. He had a desire to stay for another three or four days. At least that was what his budget permitted.

"Why?"

"It is getting somewhat boring over here," she elaborated and asked, "Don't you think so?"

Randhir had no answer to her queary. "A day or two more here will not make any difference," he said in a somewhat subdued tone.

"They do," she told him.

In order to reach Chandigarh in time for the connecting bus which would take them to Delhi well before the sun set, they decided to travel by taxi from Shimla to Chandigarh.

The taxi stopped with a jerk outside a restaurant. They had reached Kalka. "Have some refreshments," the driver told his passengers. The other three passengers went into the restaurant.

"Should I get you some tea and snacks ?" Randhir asked Smita.

"No, nothing for me," she replied. "But if you want, please go ahead." She knew tea and snacks for two was sure to cost around twenty bucks.

"No, I too don't feel like," Randhir said. "The breakfast I had in the morning is till weighing heavy on me." He was telling a lie. Unlike Smita, who had an omelette and sandwiches, he had only two toasts with thin layer of butter and a cup of tea. She doubted whether that could be playing havoc with his tommy.

They just talked about the weather at Shimla and how expensive the things were there (though they had done no shopping), as they waited for other passengers to join them.

The bus for Delhi was ready as their taxi touched the terminal at Chandigarh. It was a video-coach. The ordinary bus was to leave after about half-an-hour. "We can wait," Smita suggested. "Thirty or forty minutes are not going to make much of a difference."

Randhir imagined how the other passengers would react when they would find a newly-wedded couple travelling in an ordinary bus; not even deluxe. Smita had probably read his mind when she said, "You probably are worried about what others would think about us. After all they are not going to pay for us." Randhir was almost floored. He wondered how could the lady who three days ago looked mute, could now turn out to be so frank and forthright in her observations.

The five-hour journey from Chandigarh to Delhi was not very comfortable. They slept all through, sharing alternatively their shoulders for each other's comfort. The bus did halt at Karnal, when most of the passengers made beeline to the eating shops. But they did not move out.

It was already half-past five when the bus reached Delhi. As they came out of the terminal, Randhir headed towards the scooter stand. "Let us take the mini-bus," Smita suggested. "It just stops outside our residential block." Randhir looked at her with questioning eyes. "Now, don't get worried about what your neighbours would think when they find us walking towards our house with luggage in our hands."

They got seats to sit in the mini-bus.

"I hope you will always curse me for the sort of honeymoon I took you to," whispered Randhir, as the bus, now fully packed, weaved its way through the crowded roads.

She smiled and said, "Yes, I have a complaint to make." Randhir waited anxiously for her to come out with her statement. "I wish you should have taken me into confidence before deciding to go for it."

She explained how at Shimla she had observed him taking out a pocket diary and noting down something on it and then counting the money he had with him. That had prompted her to do a bit of spying on him. She had gone through the contents of the diary while he was in the bathroom. "I know it was indecent on my part", she said in a voice of guilt. "But then I couldn't help it." She halted for a moment and added, "I wished instead of having a honeymoon on the borrowed money, we could have postponed it for some other time. After all it was something that concerned two of us only"

Randhir could not help appreciating Smita's thoughtful views. "But don't you think this borrowed honeymoon has helped us to understand each other better ?" he queried.

Smita looked at him and smilingly nodded in affirmative.

*** *** ***

A LUMP IN THE THROAT

With great difficulty Puneet managed to reach the college. He had bruises on his face and hands. The goondas had bashed him.

But he had no regrets for what he did. Rather he patted himself for his deed. He, however, pitied all those fifty or sixty odd passengers in the bus who mutely watched the sordid drama. None came to his rescue, not even the young among them. He atleast expected that others in the bus would condemn the manner a gang of four or five goondas was harassing a young girl. But none stirred from his seat leave alone raising a protest voice. All his pleas had fallen on deaf ears.

Puneet too could have ignored. But he got worked up when despite repeated requests and protests of the girl, the gang continued to tease her. One of them had used obscene language also. Puneet stood close to the seat where the girl sat. He could gauge from her looks that she was feeling ill-at-ease. Puneet asked the gang to behave.

"Why are you poking you dirty nose ?" demanded the one who was more vocal. "Learn to respect a lady," Puneet told him.

Before he could say anything further one of the gang members had caught hold of him by his collar and slapped him. "You bastard you are trying to teach us." Other members of the gang also joined their colleague and started showering blows on Puneet. He was dragged to the rear portion of the bus and bashed. The girl had tried to intervene, but Puneet asked her not to bother. Rather he ensured that she got down from the bus at the next stop without any harm.

As the bus slowed down near a signal, Puneet was pushed out of it. His college was at a walking distance from that point.

As he entered the college he was surrounded by his classmates and friends.

"Who asked you to intervene and get bashed ?" asked one of his friends, as he was being taken to the sick room of the college.

"I just couldn't tolerate the harassment the girl was being subjected to," Puneet replied and added, "I know I was one against a gang of four or five. But thank God the girl was spared of humiliation at the hands of those rogues."

"Must be trying to impress the girl like our cine heroes," commented Krishan, who was notorious for talking loose about girls. Many a time he had received reprimands from college authorities for his involvement in eve-teasing cases. He believed that he could win over any girl with his macho-behaviour.

"Was she statistically that attractive that you were prepared to take risk ?" asked Krishan in a mischievous tone. "Had I been in your place, I would have joined the fun, *Yaar*."

Puneet gave him a furious look. "Krishan you won't understand all this. You have learnt only to play with lillies and not appreciate them." Krishan had a hearty laugh on Puneet's observation.

Puneet was given first aid and sent back to his home.

All the time Puneet was in the sick room and till his departure, Krishan continued to make derisive remarks. Puneet took no notice of them.

Krishan had forgotten the whole episode till he reached his house. His sister and parents were sitting in the drawing room and talking about the evils of eve-teasing.

The moment Krishan joined them his sister said, "Bhaiya, but for a young man I would have been in great trouble in the bus today. Poor fellow got the bashing from the goondas for my sake."

Krishan was keen to know the details. As his sister narrated the event, Krishan noted that all the details tallied with the ones provided by Puneet. He felt a lump in his throat. He wanted to rush to Puneet's house and apologise for his behaviour.

*** *** ***

AN EVENING TO REMEMBER

Devika prepared herself for the ordeal, she was to go through in the evening. It would probably be for the fifth time. Earlier four exercises had been futile. After every "seeing-the-girl" session she used to feel demoralised and dejected. In one of such moments of dejection she had even questioned herself: "Why should the boys and their parents visit our place ? Why can't we go to their houses ?" But found no answer to her query. Probably the male chauvinists thought of such a convention to satisfy their ego!

"What criteria these guys use to assess me ?" she had wondered. She was young, had a good figure and also a well-fixed up job which carried a good salary. The only minus point in her personality was probably her wheatish complexion. But her features which were sharp outweighed all minus points of her personality.

But none of the boys who had seen her so far had approved her. They didn't even have the courtesy of conveying their decisions. It was always her mother who had established contact with them to know what they had to say. Probably they had other proposals, might be even better, and could afford to pick and choose, though Devika knew that the 'dowry' was the cause of their 'rejection'. She, however had wished that the boys had expressed their 'personal' opinion and stood up against their elders in case the 'dowry' was the decisive factor. Devika had never expressed her opinion; in fact she was never asked to do so. Given a chance she would have said 'no' to at least three 'boys'. It was her widow mother's disturbed mental condition that stopped her. She didn't want to injure her feelings. She always admired her mother and the manner she managed everything with the family pension she started receiving her after her father's death. The things improved only after Devika started working.

Devika shared her mother's anxiety. After every "seeing-the-girl" show, some hopes used to be raised, till everything got fizzled out, and preparations started for the new one.

As usual Devika's mother had repeated the instructions. She was supposed to look simple but presentable. Heavy make-up was desirable. She was asked to wear sarees ("Sarees cover the extra fat of the body," she was told.), though she always felt comfortable in *Salwar-kameez*. She should bring the tray of snacks first to be followed by tea. She should remain on the scene for the `maximum' time to enable the 'boy' and those accompanying him to have a 'close' look at her.

Devika had no strength and heart to go through the same ordeal again. "It may prove to be yet another futile exercise," she thought. But she pitied her mother. She was keen that her daughter should get a good match and settle down. Devika had a college going sister, two years younger to her, and a school-going brother. Her mother was equally worried about them.

"I know Devika it is terrible to go through the whole exercise again and again," her mother had told her when she found Devika in a state of torment. "But there is no other go, my dear. I hope everything will work out well this evening."

The visit was planned for five-thirty p.m. It was already six. Devika was ready by five. The house had also been 'set'. Her mother had been to the market to get the best of the sweets and other snacks, though the experience had shown that 'they' had played no role in the exercise.

They "arrived" at quarter past seven. No apologies or explanations were offered for their late coming. The party consisted of the `boy', his parents, and three other middleaged ladies (probably `his' sisters), his brother and his wife, and about half-a-dozen kids. It looked like a picnic party.

The cold drinks wore served. The children insisted on having in bottles. Devika's mother immediately compiled with their wish. Devika came with the tray of snacks and spread them on the central table. She observed that two dozen pair of eyes were fixed on her. Devika's mother had a faint and worried smile on her lips.

As her mother served snacks, Devika went back to the kitchen to bring tea. Experienced as she was, having undergone similar exercises earlier she was not at all nervous. She had prepared herself for the worst.

Devika continued to sit on a settee with her eyes down as other talked on some irrelevant topics. She was least interested in their talk. She wanted an early end to the 'picnic'. She occasionally lifted her eyes to look at her mother. The shining beads of sweat on her forehead indicated the amount of tension and stress she was going through. Her sister who was asked to look after the lady guests, engaged them in small talk. Her ten year brother sat in a conrner with some expectancy. He too by now had got used to these 'shows'.

"Would you like to talk to the girl ?" the father asked the son. His tone sounded somewhat impertinent and rude, specially when he uttered the word 'girl'.

"Nothing in particular," the son replied casually.

"But I would like to talk to him," said Devika startling everybody. "Will you mind coming to the other room ?" She asked the boy, and almost led him to the other room.

A stony silence had descended on the scene, anxiety looming large on everybody's face.

"May be she wants to ask something that concerns her only," Devika's mother whispered by way of an explanation.

They were back after about five minutes.

"So we take your leave," announced the boy's father immediately after the son had joined the group. "We will convey our decision in about a week's time."

"Take your own time," Devika's mother said sportingly. "One should not take hasty decisions in such matters."

"Why after a week ? Why not right now ? Afterall all concerned are here," Devika asked directing her query almost at everybody present there.

Devika's outburst stunned everybody. Her mother was trembling when she pleaded with her daughter, "Probably they want to consult others."

"Then they should have brought those others also," Devika said defiantly. "If we could entertain twelve we could have entertained twenty also. And they know everything about me, and the family, and I am sure they must have done all the probing before coming over here." And then without looking around she pointedly asked the boy, "What have you to say ?" He looked at his father and paused. "It is okay from my side," he finally mumbled.

"But ......" his parents almost said in unison. Devika was quick to interrupt them. "Even if you say no, I don't mind. I am now used to such situations. But your decision must come right now."

Devika's mother still insisted, "They must be given some time to think over." But Devika was adamant. "Had I been your daughter, how would have you felt in case you were to be left in this situation of uncertainty?" a determined Devika posed the question to the boy's father. She had almost touched the right chord of the gentleman. He was immediately reminded of the sleepless nights he had spent when he was searching grooms for his two daughters, and many a time had found himself in a similar situation.

The boy and those accompanying him, in particular his parents, looked non-plussed. They were not prepared for the sort of situation they had found themselves in. There were hectic consultations among them.

"If you approve of everything," the father addressed his son, speaking somewhat in a measured tone, "we have no objection to the proposal." And probably as an after-thought added, "Rather we will be lucky to have Devika as our daughter-in-law." Devika smiled as she heard him speaking her name in a loving tone.

*** *** ***

MOMENT OF REMORSE

It was a chance meeting with Padmini that transformed Shoba. In fact it was only an encounter which lasted for about five minutes.

Shoba had gone to the Super Bazaar to buy curtain cloth for her renovated drawing room. As she was paying the bill at the cash counter, she heard somebody calling her, "Hey, Shoba". She looked back. Padmini, her school and college mate, stood before her. "Seeing you after ages !" Padmini said.

"So is with you," surprised Shoba murmured.

Shoba and Padmini had studied in the same school and had finally graduated from one of the city's prominent college. They had shared more than ten years' company of each other. Both got married immediately after they had graduated.

Even after marriage they did maintain casual contacts with each other initially. Their husbands had also met each other occasionally. But then suddenly they lost contact, especially after Padmini's husband was transferred to Bombay. Shoba did receive one or two letters from Padmini, but just couldn't reply.

They were now meeting after a gap of ten years. The years had left some marks on both. They both looked somewhat aged.

"How come you are in Delhi?" asked Shoba.

"Only I have come to Delhi. Naresh is still trying for his transfer. His parents were alone here. As Bombay's climate does not suit them, I decided to come here along with kids," explained Padmini.

"If you have time, we can go to the Coffee House," suggested Shoba. She knew Padmini was very found of coffee and the place. In college days they had visited it almost daily.

Padmini was quick to reply "No. I am sorry Shoba, I must get back home soon. My parents-in-law usually have their lunch by one; and it is already twelve-thirty."

Shoba was surprised to hear it. She couldn't believe rather. Having met each other after almost a decade, she never expected Padmini to be so curt and casual, and lacking in warmth. The manner Padmini turned down her invitation, and that too just to be on time for her parents-in-law's lunch, was beyond Shoba's reckoning.

Padmini was apologetic. "Don't mind Shoba. There is no one to look after them. Moreover I prefer serving them hot meals." And before Shoba could say anything, Padmini scribbled her address on a cash-memo and took her leave.

Shoba was stunned. She stood still as she saw Padmini rushing towards the exit gate. Her words "I prefer serving them hot meals," continued to ring in her ears. "Can Padmini be that considerate towards her husband's parents ?" she queried to herself.

Her own parents-in-law were also staying with her. Her husband being the only son they had no other place to go. But ever since her marriage she had always observed them maintaining a very low profile allowing their son and daughter-in-law to have full say in the household affairs. They talked only, if the need arose. They advised only, if asked for. They rarely interfered in what went on in the house. Still, they contributed their mite in their own way.

Her father-in-law had voluntarily taken upon himself the responsibility of leaving his grand-children at the school and also bringing them back. "There is no harm in saving some money, Atul," he had told his son, when he had expressed some apprehension at the arrangement. And lest he was misunderstood, he had added, "Moreover it provides some exercise to my body." He had also volunteered to fetch vegetables and other household nick-nacks from the market.

He had also found many a way to share his pension. "Let all the birthday parties be from my side," he had suggested. And he never forgot to bring birthday gifts. He shared the household expenses whenever Atul's sister and her family came to stay with them.

Shoba's mother-in-law was as helpful and devoted to the family as Atul's father. She was in the kitchen right from the morning assisting Shoba. "It gives me immense pleasure whenever I lend a helping hand to you Shoba," she would often say.

But for Shoba they remained non-entities. She never felt their presence. Atul too, preoccupied as he was in the affairs of his office, didn't have time to make even casual enquiries about his parents' welfare. Probably he took it granted that everything was fine with them. He had in fact left everything to Shoba's care. The old couple rarely formed a part of the talk between Atul and Shoba.

Shoba on her part never cared to know their likes and dislikes, whether it was food or other daily needs. Even the family outings and excursions were undertaken without them. Rather Atul's parents used to encourage them to take off from the rut and routine of daily life and go for picnics, etc. "This is very essential to shake off the monotony that creeps in one's life," Atul's father would advise, but quickly add, "I am talking of you my son and your wife." And his mother would further add. "And in case you want kids to be left behind, please don't hesitate we will manage them."

Shoba had known many a family where the elders were really nuisance. But she gave all the credit to her parents-in-law for attuning themselves to the environments, and that too without fuss and fury. They could have protested or snubbed for being ignored. As seniors they had every right to do so. After all they were very much a part of the family.

Shoba held Atul also responsible for all this. At least he could have been extra careful in dealing with his parents. By leaving everything to her, he had unburdened himself from all the responsibility. "They might be thinking that it was she who had tutored their son," she thought.

"Like to have anything else, Madam," the bearer's voice brought Shoba's train of thought to a sudden halt.

She jerked her head to bring herself back to the surroundings. As if she had got up from a slumber, she murmured, "No nothing. Bring the bill."

She didn't remember when she had walked into the Coffee House. She looked at her wrist watch. It was already quarter-past-one. She was there for about an hour or so.

She paid the bill and walked briskly towards the exit. " Atul must be having his lunch at this hour," she mused as she again checked time on her wrist watch. She waved at an auto-rickshaw and asked the driver to take her to Rajendra Place. Atul's office was on the third floor of one of the multi-storeyed buildings of the complex. Instead of waiting for the lift, she preferred climbing up the stairs and walked straight to Atul's cabin.

"You Shoba," surprised Atul got up to receive her and showered her with questions : "What brings you over here ? Is everything all right? Are you ..... ?"

"I have to talk something urgent to you," Shoba interrupted Atul.

"Urgent ?"

"Yes, Atul. Arrange for a week's leave and let us all go to Shimla".

"All ?"

"Yes all, including Daddy and Mummy."

Atul looked at her in disbelief.

"Don't you think Mummy and Daddy too deserve a change," she said and added, "Rather it is over-due." And before Atul could react either way, she snapped, "You better do the needful right now and come home early. We must leave tomorrow morning."

Back home Shoba's announcement that we would all be going for a short trip to Shimla surprised everyone.

"Why do you tag both of us ?" Atul's father asked.

"Old persons usually become burden on such trips," he was supported by Atul's mother.

"No Daddy without you and Mummy we are also not going."

Shoba found a glow on Atul's Daddy's face. There was glitter in Mummy's moist eyes. It seemed, though around, she had not seen these faces for years.

"Coming week is going to be a memorable one," Shoba mused to herself.

*** *** ***

NOT HER CUP OF TEA

"Hurry up Malati, we are getting late for the temple," hailed Malati's mother-in-law, Janaki.

Malati was still tying her sari. Without responding she continued to take her own time to get ready. It was somewhat intentional. She had all the mind to confront Janaki and tell her frankly that she would not pay obeisance to Rama Devi, a lady in her early forties, who held a *durbar* in the temple everyday.

Visiting the temple in the morning and attending the *durbar* was like any other routine with Janaki, and she expected others in the family also to follow it.

Malati's husband Devinder and his elder brother along with his wife Madhu without fail accompanied Janaki, though at times Malati got the impression that they did so grudgingly. There was nothing spontaneous about it. But no one dared to say 'no' to Janaki.

"Like Madhu and others you too must accompany me to the temple every morning to the temple for the *darshan* of Deviji," Malati was told by Janaki right on the day she came as a bride in the house about a month back. "You can miss anything but not this." It was almost a command that Malati was supposed not to disobey.

"Bhabi, why should all this be forced on us ?" Malati had asked Madhu.

"I have no answer to your query," Madhu had replied. "But frankly speaking I too don't like the manner we are being forced to go to the temple for the sake of Rama Devi. But I can't confront Mummy."

"But what about Bhai Sahib ?" Madhu had only grinned in answer to Malati's query.

Malati had also raised the issue with her husband. Devinder had only shrugged his shoulders and advised her not to create an unpleasant situation in the family on this frivolous matter. But for Malati it was something which neither her head nor heart was prepared to accept.

Not that Malati detested going to the temple. Neither she was an atheist in the stricter sense. What made her sick was the way she was being forced to admire and adore Rama Devi. Malati had seen many bowing and even prostrating before her. Malati had refused to do all this.

"Don't show disrespect to Deviji," Janaki had warned her. "Her curse can bring calamity. She possesses occult and supernatural powers." And to prove her point Janaki had many tales to tell; which only a person with a closed mind and no rational thinking would believe.

Malati had phoo-phooed the talk of curse and doubted whether Rama Devi possessed any such powers. "She is only trying to create a fear-psychosis to keep her hold on her followers, Mummy," Malati had rebutted.

But there was no one in the family to support her. Even her father-in-law, a scientist by profession, blindly did what Janaki directed him to do. "My child take it easy. Let us not disturb the peace of the family on such a small matter," was his reply.

To Malati it seemed that Janaki's word was last so-far-as Rama Devi was concerned. Nobody dared raise any question. "I think I alone will have to do something in this regard, "Malati had finally decided. "At least I am not going to do which does not appeal to me."

"Malati, you are delaying us also." It was again her mother-in-law. This time her tone sounded more loud and harsh.

There was some pause before Malati came out of her bedroom. "Mummy, I am not accompanying you today," Malati said. "At least not for the sake of that lady." Malati's voice almost poured venom as she spoke.

Janaki was flabbergasted. "Are you in your senses ?"

"Yes, Mummy," Malati was quick to react. "That lady does

not deserve the sort of respect you want me to show towards her.''

Janaki trembled in rage as Malati continued to speak, ''She is only cheating others and betraying their faith. And if you permit me to say Mummy, I feel she is making fool of others especially the simple ladies like you.''

''You will repent and regret for your utterances,'' Janaki sermonised.

But Malati had no regrets. She wished she should have spoken her mind the day she had seen Rama Devi in the temple. She, however, somewhat felt relieved now.

Janaki and others left for the temple without Malati. Devinder had intervened to say, ''Don't be stupid Malati ?'' Malati stood her ground. '' I have no objection in going to the temple. But don't expect me to pay any respects to that lady.''

Tension started building up in the house from that very evening. No one appreciated Malati's viewpoint. Everybody wanted her to make amends for her behaviour. But she was not prepared to relent. Rather she looked more stubborn when she asserted : ''Rama Devi doesn't deserve the sort of praises she is being showered with.''

The stalemate continued. Janaki insisted on that Malati should express regrets for her behaviour. ''She must seek apologies of Deviji for the disrespect she has shown to her,'' Janaki told others in the family when they tried to pacify her. Rather she gave an ultimatum. ''In case Malati does not act within a day or two, either she stays in the house or I.''

''I am not going to do any such thing Mummy,'' Malati had asserted and added, ''and I am prepared to pay any penalty for that.''

Malati's outburst had further annoyed Janaki. But Malati took it easy. She decided to come out with the truth about Rama Devi whatever be the consequences. And she did that at the very first opportunity that came her way.

''You know Mummy the lady whom you hold in such a high esteem is just like one of us, nothing more, nothing less,'' Malati started revealing. ''You are probably not aware that she demanded a dowry of four lakh rupees for her doctor son. She refused to accept a boy whom her daughter loved because he was from a different caste. None of her followers might be knowing that she has never bothered to care for her husband who is a chronic asthmatic patient."

Everybody sat with gaping mouth as they listened to Malati. Malati continued, "That lady claims that she possesses occult and such like powers. If that is so, why her elder daughter who is married for last twelve years, is still issueless."

Malati paused and looked straight at her mother-in-law and said, "In fact Mummy I hold you in much high an esteem than that lady. You accepted me as your daughter-in-law knowing well that I belong to not-so-rich a family and supported Devinder when he refused to take any dowry. You raised no objection when Bhai Sahib decided to marry a girl from a non-brahmin family. I have more regard for Daddy who in addition to his job is giving free tuition to the needy students."

Janaki felt elated as she listened to Malati. The bitterness which she was carrying for her daughter-in-law had almost started vanishing.

"But how come Malati you know so much about Rama Devi and her family ?" asked Devinder.

"Because her younger daughter was my class-mate and a very close friend and the girl whom Rama Devi had refused to accept as her daughter-in-law was none else but me," Malati talked in low halting tone.

There was almost a chorus of "Is that so ?"

*** *** ***

A DAY TO REMEMBER

Shankar took out the duster from the drawer and cleaned the chair and table

It was a routine for him. He did that mechanically everyday before starting day's work.

He changed the date on the table calender. It was thirtieth day of November. There was something special about the date. He suddenly remembered that it was his wife's birthday.

He cursed himself for not having remembered in the morning. He could have surprised her by wishing her many happy returns of the day. He could have taken off and be with her.

But his mornings were so busy and hectic that he just managed to reach office on time. Travelling by bus from his residence to office itself took more than an hour.

He was sure that even his wife might not be remembering that it was her birthday today.

Ever since their marriage three years ago he had been thinking of celebrating her birthday. He had been thinking of holding a small party and inviting some of his close friends and relations. But every time he remembered about it only after the thirtieth November.

Last year when he had aplogised for having forgotten to wish her and present her with a birthday gift, she had told him, "I am not a small kid that I should feel sorry for not getting a gift."

But Shankar had felt guilty and vowed to remember it the following year.

He knew of many colleagues and friends who always remembered to present special gifts to their spouses on their birthdays. The small courtesies like wishing and presenting the gifts go a long way in cementing the bonds of love between the couples, he had read in some journal.

"I must give her a surprise today," Shankar thought. His right hand instantaneously went in his pocket. He had seven rupees. The sum would not bring any worthwhile present, leave alone a memorable one.

He became philosophical in his thoughts. "Thirtieth is no date to take birth. For salaried people like us only first week of the month is the best. Had it been the first or second of the month, he would have given her a gift, even a valuable one." He sighed.

Shanker thought of borrowing some money. He had financial dealings only with Ram Lal. He had very often taken small loans from him, especially during the last days of months.

Shankar picked up strength and went to Ram Lal's seat.

"Today is thirtieth."

"Yes, you are right," Ram Lal replied casually.

"Can you spare some money? I want to buy a ...," Shankar Lal spoke haltingly.

"You want to buy what?"

"A gift for my wife. Today is her birthday," Shankar ejaculated.

Ram Lal, who till then was inattentive, suddenly found himself in a reflective mood, "I am sorry Shankar, I cannot spare money today. I have about fifty rupees. But I have to take my wife for an x-ray. The money may be just enough for it." Ram Lal's voice sounded his helplessness.

Shankar knew that being the month-end, like him, others in the office might be sailing in the same boat. He decided to buy a gift with the money he had. Let it be only a token of love, he finally thought.

He would rather walk back to his residence and save on the bus fare. He decided to miss his usual quota of tea and snacks. He must save whatever possible, he murmured to himself.

He spent rest of the day restlessly and could not concentrate on his work. Now and then he turned and saw the slow moving needles of the wall clock and checked also the time on his wrist watch. He almost lived with the thoughts of Kamani's birthday and the present he would give.

At last it was all over. He got up and without looking at any of his colleagues — he wanted no interruptions — he walked out of the office.

As Shankar walked in the bazar, he thought of many items which he could buy as gift.

He entered a general merchandise shop and asked the shopkeeper to show him some brass rings. Finally he purchased a ring with ''K'' engraved on it, and got it wrapped with coloured craft paper.

He started walking with a brisk pace.

''What a thoughtful husband 1 may prove to be.'' He felt flattered for buying a present for Kamani.

He was so absorbed in his thoughts, he did not realise that he had reached his home.

Kamani was in the kitchen. He rushed in and exclaimed, ''Sorry darling, I forgot to .....''

Before he could speak further Kamani interrupted him, ''I know you would forget. Didn't I tell you in the morning that today was the last day for the ration, and it is a already seven-thirty. The ration shop might have closed by now.'

Shankar stood still as his hand played with the gift in his pocket.

*** *** ***

BEYOND GLITZ AND GLAMOUR

As usual, Arvind was somewhat late in reaching the Bombay Central station to catch the Rajadhani Express which was leaving at 5.00 p.m. He checked the time on his wrist watch, as he disposed of the taxi. It was ten minutes to five.

"It is one hell of a job to locate the right bogie and the seat even in an air-conditioned chair-car," he mused as he strode towards the train. He passed by a stream of people, almost bumping into them.

"Here it is," he said as he stood before a compartment and hurriedly checked the list pasted at the entrance. He rushed in and located his seat. As he settled down he observed the seat next to him was still vacant. The engine had already blown its first whistle. He looked around to see whether there was somebody still struggling to locate his or her seat. There was no one. The whole compartment looked full. There were a few others like him who could not reach on time, he thought to himself.

The train had started moving. "Excuse me, please," a lady's voice addressed Arvind "The seat next to yours is mine." He turned back to have a look at the lady. Her face looked familiar. Without putting much strain on his memory, he recalled that she was no one else but Shikha. He squeezed his legs to allow her to move to her seat.

Arvind had another look at the lady from the corner of his eyes. She was Shikha, his college friend and class mate. Shikha was not a shade of what she used to be. The facial glow had almost faded. She was hunched at the shoulders because of protruding bones. The eyes which used to be armoury of her beauty, had dark circles beneath them.

She was certainly not the Shikha whom Arvind had known. She used to be the rage of the college. She had even been crowned as the college beauty queen. Many in the college were eager to seek her out. The extra-attention and indulgence that she received from others had gone to her head. She became very arrogant and egotistical.

Arvind, on the other hand, was popular for his debating qualities and stage performances. He had earned quite a name for himself by winning many prizes in the inter-college and inter-university competitions. He too was always eager to seek Shikha's company. He made many efforts to be friendly with her. She had not only ignored, but at times also snubbed him.

Arvind had once requested her to act in one of his plays. She had felt offended and told him off, curtly, - "How dare you ask me? Do you expect me to act in :your nautankis?" She had fumed.

Arvind, however, had continued to yearn for Shikha's company and friendship. An infatuation for her had always lingered deep down within him. But Shikha's attitude of "I-care-two-hoots-for-you" had made him sad.

"I only like the company of smarties," she had told him contemptuously when he had invited her over for a cup of tea in the university cafe.

Shikha was always spotted in the company of the boys who had motor-bikes and cars to ride on and hosted parties in five star hotels at the drop of a hat. Arvind had once warned Shikha about the sort of company she was keeping.

"They are all rowdies and rogues. I wish you would keep aloof from such people." Her reaction was wild: "None of your business man, whether I move around with saints or rowdies. Who are you to advice me?" She had retorted scathingly.

"I am your well-wisher, Shikha."

"Well-wisher, my foot," Shikha had snapped back at him.

That was probably the last Arvind had seen of Shikha, though he had been hearing many spicy and scandalous stories about her.

One day the college had been agog with the news that Shikha had eloped with Sameer, a local businessman's son. The guess was that they had gone to Bombay where Sameer's uncle was a film-producer. Sameer had probably exploited Shikha's weakness for the glamour of the cine-world.

Calm had returned to the compartment. Now tea was being served. Arvind observed that the lady was glancing through a film-magazine. She was certainly not reading. Her changing facial expressions indicated that she was not at peace with herself. Something was surely disturbing her a lot. .She didn't look up once towards Arvind. "Maybe she had not recognised me", he thought. "I may be wrong in trying to place her."

"Excuse me . . . are you . . . ?" He drew the lady's attention. "Yes, Arvind," the lady interrupted him. "I am Shikha. I had recognised you the moment I saw you but could not pick up the courage to talk to you."

Arvind was glad that he was not wrong. He had a close look at Shikha once again. She certainly looked a sick woman. Arvind was seeing her after about three years. The intervening period had taken its toll on her looks and charm.

"Are you not well?" It was Arvind who started the conversation. Shikha did not answer but had a wane smile on her lips. She avoided Arvind's stare and continued to look down. "I had never hoped that I would ever meet you again," Arvind continued. "Today's meeting had come as a pleasant surprise."

"The same is also true of me" Shikha responded cautiously.

"I had come to Bombay on an official tour," Arvind said in order to involve Shikha in further conversation. "I am working as a media-executive in an advertising agency in Delhi. In fact I come to Bombay very often. I knew you were supposed to be in Bombay. Sameer had promised to get you a break in the films through his uncle."

Shikha stirred in her seat for the first time. "It was all a fraud, a lie," she spoke in an agitated tone. "The man was only a distant relation of Sameer. As a matter of fact it was a well-laid out trap just to exploit me. In the name of screen tests, both Sameer and his so-called uncle played havoc with my life. Finally, Sameer deserted me. I was too scared to go back to my parents; probably didn't have the guts to face them. They would have even disowned me. I did many odd jobs for a living. But with my sort of background, I was exploited every where." She paused to give herself some breathing time.

"But Arvind, to be frank with you, all these years I felt insecure. I wanted somebody who could provide protection and a sense of security to me. A friend who would truly share my moments of grief and loneliness."

Arvind observed that tears were trickling down her cheeks. He didn't realise when his hand had grabbed her's. She suddenly composed herself and said, "But I am determined to come out of this self-created hell. That is why, I have accepted the job of a hostel warden in a Delhi school. An old teacher had helped me to get this job. While in Delhi, I will make a sincere effort to win over my parents."

She suddenly stopped talking. It seemed that she felt easy and relaxed. Probably after years she had found somebody with whom she could talk so frankly and in such a forthright manner.

"But everything is not lost Shikha," Arvind consoled her. "You can, if you want, start a new chapter in your life. I am there to help you. I still love you."

Shikha looked at Arvind with dismay and disbelief.

"Even after knowing whatever I have been through?" she said in a questioning tone.

"Yes, Shikha, I still love you," assured Arvind. "I am prepared to marry you," he added.

"Will your parents accept me?" asked Shikha apprehensively.

"I don't care as long as you are by my side. We have to stand by each other, whatever the consequences."

Tears again started rolling down Shikha's eyes. "I am grateful to you, Arvind, for giving some meaning to my life and existence," she said as she rested her head on Arvind's shoulder.

The stewards were getting ready to serve dinner. They had both come home.

*** *** ***

CHAND

She was back in the building. Her return, after a year, was taken as a matter of fact. None of the inmates was surprised to see her there. Nobody showed any anxiety to meet her.

Even the mistress, when informed of her return, displayed a vain smile, almost conveying: "I knew she would come back."

Chand went straight to the room she was occupying a year ago. Everything there was in the same order. Nothing had changed.

A year had made no difference to the place. Only the corner in the room, which belonged to her, was being occupied by some other girl.

Salama and Saloni, who were sharing the room with her, were very much there

"How are you, Chanderlekha?" Salama asked her.

"Chanderlekha" sounded familiar to her ears. She was known in the building only by that name.

The name "Chand" was given to her by the journalist who had visited the building to do an investigative story on prostitution.

"Chand can be a Hindu, a Muslim or even a Sikh." That was how he had started the series of articles on prostitutes and their woes.

Prostitution knows no religion. The visitors to these market places of flesh too do not know any religion. Their aim is to enjoy their evenings and nights with any girl without bothering for her caste and creed.

"A staunch pandit, who is seen doing puja in the temple during the day, visits these girls and enjoys their company." And the journalist had listed some prominent residents of the city who were frequenting these places.

The story had created a sensation. "Chanderlekha" had become "Chand."

The publicity — her picture was carried on the front page of the newspaper — had gone to her head. Despite the warnings of the mistress, she had supplied all sorts of information to the journalist.

"The *akhbarwala* is not going to take you as his bride," the mistress had told her. But she had ignored the warning.

"You are afraid because you have been exposed and your business will be affected. Babu will not let me down," Chanderlekha had boasted.

But she was proved wrong. The business was dull only initially. The special police post, established in the area after the publication of the report, was effective only for a day or two.

The mistress had arranged to establish close contact with the incharge of the post and everything was smooth thereafter.

But, for Chanderlekha, nothing was smooth after she walked out of the building. She carried on her a stamp that identified her.

The sensation, created by the story about her and her profession, made no difference to her.

Whether it was the police lock-up where she stayed for 3 days or Nari Niketan — where she stayed for about a year — she was given a treatment that was no different from what she received, while in the building.

The SHO had shamelessly asked favours from her. She had refused, resisted, even abused him for his behaviour.

He had taunted her. "Nothing can remove the scars you carry. You can never, never be a Sita or a Savitri."

To make her yield to the wishes of the SHO, she was starved and tortured, till she was left with no strength to resist.

Nari Niketan was another hell for Chand. Sunita Behn, a social worker, who looked after the abode of the destitutes, was no different from the mistress.

In the garb of a social worker, a reformer, a helper of the helpless, she asked the residents of the Niketan to do what in the building the mistress told them to.

The mistress had suddenly gone high in Chand's esteem. At least she was no hypocrite. She had boldly and plainly spoken about herself and her profession, when the journalist had interviewed her. She did not mince words, but called a spade a spade.

"If I have to live in hell only, the mistress's hell is better than a place where everything looks far from reality," Chand had finally decided.

She ran away from the rescue home and was back in the building. Back in the surroundings which no more appeared repulsive to her.

"I have come back, Auntie." Chand stood before the mistress.

"So what?" The mistress was indifferent, indignant.

"I have come back to work for you."

"But I have now another girl in your place. There is no spare cot for you. And who knows, that *akhbarwala* may come again and create problems for me."

Chand very much wanted to prostrate before the mistress and seek her forgiveness. But the mistress looked determined to send her out. She had already sent a word to the policeman at the post to take back Chand to the rescue home.

"Havaldar Sahib, take this bitch away and tell that *akhbarwala* to write another story on her."

The mistress took out a 100 rupee note and handed it over to the Havaldar. "This is your *baksheesh*."

The Havaldar flashed a broad smile, as she held Chand by her shoulder. He almost dragged her out.

Next day, there was a 3-line report in the news-in-brief column of a newspaper that the body of a girl, reported to be from the red-light area, was found near the banks of the Yamuna. The Police was making further enquiries.

It was the same paper which had carried Chand's story on its front page.

*** *** ***

THE COWARD

Nandini was in two minds. Should she or should she not appear in the court as a witness ? Amar's wife had lodged a complaint with the police that she was being ill-treated by her husband and in-laws for bringing insufficient dowry.

She had named Nandini as one of the witnesses. Nandini knew that her statement would prove crucial. Nandini had almost erased from her mind, the days spent in Amar's company. The day he had conveyed his decision that he had yielded to his parents' wishes, she had ceased thinking about him. Nandini was not surprised when the police had approached her to appear in the court as a prosecution witness. "A coward will always remain a coward," she thought as she recalled the last meeting she had with Amar.

"You see Nandini.... I just couldn't say no to my parents," he had told her and added, "I confess I was not able to bring them round to my views."

"Couldn't you tell them that you would like to marry a girl of your choice and that too without any dowry?" Nandini had retorted in anger, looking straight in his eyes. "Probably you didn't have the guts."

His silence had proved her charge. That was their last meeting. Nandini had eventually reconciled to a life without Amar.

It was probably an irony of fate that the debate on dowry in the university had brought them closer. It was by no means, love-at-first-sight. It was the coming together of two individuals sharing similar convictions and ideals.

Amar's performance in the debate had impressed Nandini. He had spoken against dowry and criticised the dowry seekers. "The evil of dowry can only be fought by the youngsters," he had argued and roared, "all those who think the brides are for burning should be hanged."

He had spoken for about forty-five minutes and sounded sincere in his arguments. At least Nandini had thought so. He was adjudged the best debater.

"Congratulations, Amar," Nandini had got hold of him at the university gate.

"Thanks."

"You spoke so well and convincingly that you almost swept the audience off their feet".

"Including you," a smiling Amar had remarked.

The casual introductory meeting had blossomed into intimacy. They had started meeting frequently. The venues were the university coffee house and the library.

Amar was a research scholar and was writing a doctoral thesis on "Social Reforms and the Role of Women."

"Amar, I feel you have selected a very wrong subject for your Ph.D.," Nandini had once told Amar. "You may not be able to do justice to it." And without waiting for Amar's reaction, she had said, "Our society is still male-dominated and the women play no role. Or should I say the women are not allowed to play any role?"

She had deliberately broached the subject. She wanted to probe Amar and was keen to know his views on marriage and dowry. "Take the case of dowry. Don't you think girls and their parents have no option in this regard?" she had pointedly asked him.

Amar had avoided a direct reply. He had merely said, "It depends." For the first time Nandini had got a glimpse of a person who was not sure of himself.

It seemed he had some mental reservations. Probably his family background had something to do with his thinking. Amar was the only son of a prominent businessman.

Nandini was an orphan and depended wholly on elder brother who was an assistant in a government office. He had warned her to tread cautiously on the path that she had chosen for herself. "Nandini, the realities of life are different from what you talk, discuss and debate," he had told her.

But Nandini had full faith in Amar. She was sure he would stand by her. But still she wanted him to be straightforward and forthright and not beat about the bush as he had been doing whenever Nandini had tried to question him about their marriage.

"Amar have you talked to your parents regarding our marriage?" She had confronted Amar with a query which he had been trying to avoid. It was a straight query that demanded a straight answer.

"Marriage as such is no problem, Nandini. It is ..." He was hesitant.

"It is what?" She was anxious to know.

"It is the status of the two families. My parents want me to marry a girl. ..." He was probably not finding the right words to express himself. He again started speaking in a voice which was feeble and low. "You know Nandini ..."

Shocked, Nandini was not prepared to listen to him any further. In fact she needed no explanation. It would have made no difference to her. Reality had dawned on her. Amar stood completely exposed. From that day onwards she had started distancing herself from him.

Then one day Nandini had come to know that Amar had finally succumbed to the wishes of his parents and decided to marry a girl of their choice. Nandini had no regrets. She had only pitied Amar.

"He will never learn to stand up for himself, be it love or marriage," she had mused to herself.

Nandini had known Amar's fiancee, Neena. They were classmates in the school. Neena's father was the rich owner of a chain of fast-food restaurants in the city.

"Amar's parents are a greedy lot," Nandini had warned Neena when they had a chance meeting, in a department store. "And about Amar less said the better. He has no guts to stand against his parents."

"So what ? My Dad has plenty of money to silence anybody," Neena had casually said.

"I am speaking from my experience Neena and want you to think twice before you take a final decision".

"Probably for you, the grapes were sour Nandini," Neena had taunted. Nandini had taken the remark very sportingly.

Nandini had forgotten about the whole affair, till Neena sought an urgent meeting with her.

"Nandini my marriage is on the rocks," she had told her and added, "I am going through hell." She narrated how Amar's parents had been ill-treating her for not fulfilling some of their demands, though her father had given her a good dowry and spent a lot on the marriage.

"But the tragedy is that Amar says nothing. He doesn't even protest. He just watches mutely." Neena was bitter.

Nandini had cut her short. "It does not matters to me now."

"I want your help."

"In what way can I help you ?"

"I have lodged a complaint against Amar and his parents. In fact I'm seeking separation. Your statement can strengthen my case," Neena had pleaded with Nandini.

Nandini had only said, "I will think it over." She needed time to make up her mind.

Cowards like Amar must be exposed. So that, others too were not cheated by their hollow talk, Nandini decided finally. Though she had no sympathies for Neena, she didn't want to miss the opportunity provided to expose hypocrites like Amar.

*** *** ***

NEIGHBOURLY YOURS

If Vasudevan Iyer had had his way, he would have liked only a Tamilian, and that too, an Iyer, to be his neighbour. But he had no choice. The clerks, sitting in the Estate Office, were the sole arbitrators. They blindly allotted the Government flats to any Tom, Dick or Harry, with little consideration for the persons who were to acquire them, as their neighbours.

Vasudevan found himself in a similar situation when his wife, Padma, informed him that some Khanna, working in the Home Ministry, was to occupy the opposite flat.

Vasudevan was shocked. "So it will be a Punjabi nuisance that we have to confront now," he commented.

He carried a very poor opinion about the Punjabis. "They encroach upon your privacy, and try to be overfriendly even if you want to avoid them," he was very often heard telling others.

An upset Vasudevan forewarned his wife and the children. "Do not try to get very close to that family. Never give an impression that we are eager to seek their friendship," he told them.

"Why do you paint everybody with the same brush?" questioned Vasudevan's son, Krishnan, a junior executive in a private firm. "You can find good and bad people everywhere and anywhere."

Vasudevan was taken aback. He looked piercingly at his son.

"I have a good number of Punjabi friends in my college too, and they are all nice and good," remarked Radha, Vasudevan's college-going-daughter.

Knowing that Vasudevan had never liked anybody to challenge him, Padma admonished both Krishnan and Radha, and averted an argument.

The day the Khannas occupied their flat, it became clear that theirs was an outgoing family. The manner in which they took the initiative and visited and introduced themselves to their immediate neighbours, was appreciated by all.

But Vasudevan took exception to their visit. "See their audacity," he told his wife, immediately after Mr. and Mrs. Khanna and their two children had left their flat. "They came uninvited."

But Padma appreciated their gesture. "It was nice of them to have come and seen us," she said. Both Krishnan and Radha agreed with their mother. Vasudevan simply looked helpless.

The days passed. The Khannas, both seniors and juniors, were proving to be very amenable, their helpful nature winning them many friends. Padma, Krishnan and Radha had started admiring them. "They are really very nice," was the opinion of the threesome.

But Vasudevan's reaction was very sharp. "To begin with, they behave like this always. But once they win over your confidence, they will be sitting on your neck.'

Notwithstanding Vasudevan's opinion about the Khanna family, the ladies of the two houses and the youngsters started meeting each other very often. While Padma and Shanti exchanged notes on the recipes of the north and south, the youngsters talked of movies, literature and sport.

The "feasts" and "treats" of makki-ki-roti and sarson-ka-saag and sambar-dosa became routines with the two families, minus, of course, Vasudevan. Once or twice, Pawan Kumar, the elder Khanna, requested Vasudevan also to join the others on such occasions; but he flatly refused.

The feasts and get-togethers brought both Krishnan and Kamini, who was doing a vocational course, closer. Radha and Nihal, Kamini's younger brother, played supportive roles in the affair which, ultimately bloomed into a deep romance.

Vasudevan was the first to detect the affair. He decided to nip it in the bud. He called Pawan Kumar to his office and gave him a piece of his mind.

"But we have to handle them with care," Pawan Kumar

cautioned Vasudevan. "These days, youngsters are a determined lot and do just as they please."

Vasudevan took exception to Pawan Kumar's observation. "That means you have been encouraging your daughter to indulge in all this," he accused hotly.

"It is not that, Vasudevan Sahib," explained Pawan Kumar. "Certain things just happen, whether you like them or not. I take a practical view of everything."

Vasudevan was not prepared to listen to Pawan Kumar's sermon. "I have not called you to listen to your lecture. I just want an early end to the affair, 'he told him.

"Let us seek the help of our wives," suggested Pawan Kumar. Vasudevan agreed.

The ladies, it seemed, did have an inkling of what was going on, but thinking that it was teenagers' crush, had chosen to ignore it. Only when they were informed about its seriousness, did they become alert.

"Tell your son to stop all this — and also that girl from the opposite flat not to meet him anymore," Vasudevan told Padma.

But both Krishnan and Kamini were determined in their resolve to marry, and told their mothers that nothing could stop them. They had full support from Radha and Nihal.

But Padma and Shanti were perturbed about the fall-out. "In case, they ignore us and go ahead with their marriage plans, we will all be cutting a sorry figure," a worried Shanti told Padma. The latter held the same view.

Having taken a tough stance, it had become very difficult for the elders, specially Vasudevan, to retrace their steps. They did not know how to resolve the matters. They had either to give in, or keep away from what the youngsters planned to do.

But, the youngsters served an ultimatum to the seniors by fixing marriage date and issuing the invitation cards in the name of their parents. With their names getting tagged, the elders were left with no option but to participate in the marriage. At least, their physical presence had become a must.

On the wedding day, Vasudevan and Padma, in their colourful native attires, and Pawan Kumar, in his typical Punjabi headgear and Shanti, in salwar-kameez, stood at the entrance to receive the guests.

The youngsters highly appreciated the elders' participation and expressed their gratitude to all of them, and to Vasudevan, in particular. Vasudevan, forgetting the old bitterness, was in the best of moods.

Like the menu, which had all the choicest from both the north and south, the marriage ceremonies were also a delightful mixture of the two cultures.

But the greatest surprise of the function was probably reserved for the end. As Kamini bent down to touch the feet of Krishnan's parents, she addressed them in Tamil.

"How come, you are addressing us in Tamil, Kamini?" asked a surprised Vasudevan.

"Krishnan taught me," she replied.

"But no one taught me Punjabi. I just picked it up," interjected Krishnan as he addressed Kamini's parents in his broken Punjabi.

Vasudevan could not help hugging his daughter-in-law, and his half-baked Punjabi son.

*** *** ***

THE RAT RACE

Left to himself Nand Lal, as in previous years, would have sent only a Diwali greeting card to his managing director. But this time his wife insisted on his taking a gift instead.

"Cards are no way of greeting the bosses," Jaya had advised him. "Especially the ones who matter. They get thousands of such cards and throw them in wastepaper basket without even registering the names of the senders in their minds."

Nand Lal was inclined to agree with his wife. Afterall every year he had been greeting the MD and other senior officers through most expensive cards with the best messages therein. But barring stereo-type and smile-less 'thanks', Nand Lal never got anything in 'return.' Atleast nothing that gave him personal or professional satisfaction. Even occasional acknowledgments by a senior or two were mere scraps of paper for him.

There were many in the office who never missed an opportunity to take gifts to their seniors, be it Diwali or Durga Puja. For them these festivals were only an excuse to get close to the superiors. Some even kept a calender of the festivals which some of the seniors celebrated.

That good-for-nothing Gurbachan, never forgot to greet the MD, a Keralite, on Onam. He would specially buy a sari for MD's wife and deliver at his place on the day. Once or twice he had taken gifts for his teenage children also. Probably all this had helped him in getting two out-of-turn promotions; and superseding Nand Lal, who continued to hold the position of a junior assistant, the post he had joined the office to start with.

Nand Lal had once taunted Gurbachan. "Do you know the significance of Onam," he had asked him. "Who cares so long as what I do pleases the boss," Gurbachan had replied in a tone that gave clear indication of his motives.

Like Gurbachan, Muthuswamy, an orthodox Tamilian, always made it a point to greet the Chief Sales Executive, a Punjabi, on Baisakhi and Lori. The Pongal provided another opportunity to Muthuswamy to invite and present gifts to the seniors who mattered. And the indebted seniors were always keen to reward Muthuswamy. His rise from a salesman's job to that of a sales supervisor never came as a surprise to Nand Lal.

Sudhakar, a staunch Hindu, always remembered to walk in Chief Financial Advisor Mirza's cabin and hug him and convey *Eid Mubarak*. Knowing Mirza's weakness for foreign scents, he always carried a bottle of the best available imported scent with him. A ledger clerk Sudhakar was now an accountant.

But the most classic example was set by Banerjee Babu. Without spending a naya paisa he managed to grab the Administrative Officer's post. Every year he manipulated to become the convener of the Durga Puja Celebrations Committee of his locality and invited General Manager Roy to act as the chief guest. But for this gesture Banerjee would have continued to be the godown incharge.

Not that only juniors and middle-level colleagues of Nand Lal excelled in sycophancy. The seniors were also very much in the race.

The General Manager never forgot to send "complimentary" tickets, but of course paid for, to the MD for the gala celebration of new year eves in a five star hotel. This guaranteed complete freedom of working for the GM. None ever questioned his actions, administrative or otherwise.

All these thoughts came to Nand Lal's mind as he weighed Jaya's suggestion of taking a Diwali gift to the MD's house. He probably was the only one yet to learn the tricks that others had so cunningly played to corner all sorts of benefits.

"In a way Jaya is right," Nand Lal mused to himself, as he finally decided to buy a gift.

"What gifts should we get ?" he asked Jaya.

"You should know it better," she replied. "By now you should have known his likes and dislikes." Nand Lal was almost caught napping. He had never cared to go into all these details. He had always confined himself to his work.

"Still you can guide me," he said. Jaya thought over it and came out with the list. "Let us get terrycot *Kurta payjama* for your MD and Banarasi saree for his wife. For the daughter and son we can get jeans." Nand Lal agreed with the proposal.

A tidy sum of around two thousand rupees went into the purchase. They were neatly packed and with the greeting card tagged on the packet both Nand Lal and Jaya arrived at MD's house.

They were received by the MD and his wife in the drawing room, which overflowed with gifts, baskets full of fruits and packets of sweets and other assorted eatables.

"Why did you take the trouble of bringing all this ?" they asked.

"Just a token of love, Sir," a hesitant Nand Lal replied.

"Anyway thank you very much," interjected MD's wife. Both Nand Lal and Jaya felt relieved.

"What would you like to have ?"

"Nothing Sir," Nand Lal was prompt in responding. " We just had our breakfast. And today being Diwali it will be eating all through the day."

A sudden silence descended in the room. Nand Lal did not know what else he should talk to prolong his stay.

It was the MD who broke the silence. "You see Gurbachan came last night and presented a VCR. Probably one of his uncles is manufacturing the VCRs. The children are damn happy to have it. They were pestering me to get one."

Nand Lal was shocked. He knew it for certain that Gurbachan had no uncle, leave alone one having an electronics factory. Gurbachan himself owned only a black and white television set.

"So Gurbachan is again one up over others," thought Nand Lal, as he and his wife took leave of the MD and his wife:

Next day when Nand Lal reached the office, there was a strong rumour of Gurbachan being promoted as the regional manager for north zone.

*** *** ***

STIR IN STILLNESS

It had rained without break for more than two hours. Like an exhausted and tired woman who had delivered a child, everything stood still. Nothing moved. The dripping from leaves, the croaks of frogs, the chirriping of birds, occasionally, did cause some disturbance.

For Amit it was not the first rain. He had seen many such rains since his joining the forest service 10 years ago. He was accustomed to the forest life. Perhaps there was no escape.

Reading fiction and listening to music — ghazal was his weakness — were his pastime. He had a very good collection of cassettes. Whenever he visited a city, he made it a point to go to a music shop and ask for the latest arrivals.

As usual, his two-in-one played his favourite Chitra-Jagjit numbers. Eyes closed and hands playing on the arms of the chair, he enjoyed it.

He waited for Sarita to join him. It was the time for evening tea and Rawat, driver-cum-cook, had twice sought Amit's permission. "Wait, let Mem Sahib come," he told Rawat.

Rawat was with him right from the beginning. Being well-informed about the forests of the area, he had been a great asset to Amit on his tours. Though officially he was the driver for the jeep provided to Amit, he offered to cook and continued to do so even after Sarita had joined Amit after marriage eight years ago. He, his wife and two sons were almost a part of the family. Rawat's wife provided a good company to Sarita at a place where it was needed the most.

Sarita came out and pushed the chair close to the table. The screeching sound disturbed Amit. "Rawat bring the tea," she said.

Rawat was quick as if waiting in the wings. He kept the tray on the table and waited for the instructions. "I will prepare," Sarita told him.

Amit always enjoyed this hour. Breakfast was taken in a hurry and lunch in office. This was the time he felt fully relaxed.

This was also the hour when Amit and Sarita exchanged notes. Amit told her about his experiences in forests and office, and she talked about the new recipe or the new dress she had tried during the day. She was expert in both. After graduation, she had done short courses in dress designing and cookery. She always had a feeling of fulfilment when she fabricated a new design. Her two sisters also depended on her for the clothes they needed for their children.

Sarita poured tea into cups and made first for Amit. Both sipped from their cups. Amit was still absorbed in a Chitra-Jagjit number. Sarita looked vacantly at the steam that emitted from her cup.

Sarita broke the silence. "A letter has come from Bombay. Didi is again in the family way," she said.

"The third time," he said in a matter-of-factly tone.

Sarita nodded as she gulped down the tea. Her thoughts went awry: " Is he taunting me?"

"Won't the third child be a burden?" she asked. There was a feeling of frustration in her query. Amit only smiled.

Her elder sister's marriage had taken place only a year earlier than her's and she was pregnant for the third time, whereas Sarita yearned for a child. Even her younger sister who was married about five years ago was a mother of two kids.

For the first two years Amit and Sarita did not bother. But, later on they did get worried. They had been consulting medical experts, well-known gynaecologist, visiting peers and seers, and tantriks. But their wish remained unfulfilled.

Once or twice they did think of adoption. But Amit did not favour it; at least not anyone from among his or her relations. He was not willing to adopt an orphan either. "That is just not possible," he had told her.

But at the same time both yearned for a child. At times their relations got strained on this score, compelling Amit to over-indulge in drinks and sending Sarita into moods of seclusion.

"Should I get you some more tea?" she asked.

"Yes," he said, as he got up to change the cassette. He had increased the volume. Now it was Ghulam Ali.

Sarita made the cup and handed over to Amit.

"Didi wants to undergo an abortion and wants us to help in the matter," said Sarita, again touching on the sister's letter.

"Why an abortion?" asked Amit.

"Maybe Jeejaji does not want the third child."

"Is she specific about it or are you making a guess only?"

Sarita had no explanation. Her sister's letter had only indicated that she wanted an abortion. Whether it was her husband's wish, Sarita was not sure. However, her sister was specific that she would not like her husband to know about it.

"But why the poor creature be killed?" Amit queried, but was quick-to add: "We can offer to adopt the child."

"We?" Sarita repeated the word emphatically, and looked piercingly at Amit almost disbelieving him. He the one who had all been opposing adoption should be concerned about a "creature" who was yet to land on this earth. "Did he father the child?" she questioned herself.

Suspicion engulfed her. Her mind travelled back to his tour of Bombay two months back, where he had gone to attend a seminar. He had decided to go alone. There was nothing unsual in it. Earlier also he had left her alone in the care of Rawat and his wife. But on this particular tour she had insisted on accompanying him. She had not visited her elder sister for a couple of years. Amit's tour provided her an opportunity which she did not want to miss. But he had insisted that he would go alone.

"It is a very hectic tour. Just a-touch-and-go-sort of," he had told her.

"Probably he had other things in his mind in his stubborn refusal to take her along," Sarita thought as she reflected back on his Bombay visit.

On his return from Bombay also Amit had displayed an

extraordinary exuberance in his behaviour, which, looked strange to Sarita. He had always behaved in an even manner, never touching the extreme. But she was well aware of his habit of getting astray in the company of other women specially in his state of drunkenness. Sometimes he had been unabashed, in his flirtations, not sparing even Rawat's wife. All this weighed on her mind when she heard him telling about adoption.

"Did he make her sister a victim of his lust? Or did she submit herself to his flirtation? Or did both became party to each other's desire?" All these questions came to her mind as she reminisced about his Bombay visit.

"Should I get some more tea Mem Sahib?" asked Rawat halting her train of thought.

"No."

She looked around. Amit had already moved in. The two-in-one was still playing Ghulam Ali. The frogs' croaks were now more pronounced. It had started raining again, disturbing the stillness of the sorroundings. The chilly winds made her uneasy. As she got up to move in, she took an instant decision not to reply to her sister's letter.

*** *** ***

MOMENT OF TRUTH

The letter upset both Badri Prasad and his wife Basanti Devi. They did not expect their son to be so indifferent in his reply. Afterall, one must be somewhat discreet in writing, especially when a son writes to his parents. But Raman, their younger son, was not only curt and terse, in his reply, but also evasive, cleverly missing the central point.

Ever since the arrival of the letter two days back, its contents had been the main talking point between Badri Prasad and his wife. Sitting on the breakfast table, Badri Prasad again referred to the letter and expressed his anguish. He wanted to send a reply that would have meant almost snapping all the ties that existed till now.

"Will the curry of potatoes be alright for the lunch?" asked Basanti to pacify an agitated Badri Prasad.

"Everything is alright with me," he replied without looking at her. As a matter of fact, he had never been fussy about food. After his retirement, he had changed himself altogether. He ate whatever was served to him. He had no heart to comment on the food so painstakingly prepared by Basanti despite her indifferent health. Rather he had all praise for her. All through she had been nice and considerate, never giving him any chance to grumble.

But it now pained Badri Prasad to see her suffer in silence. At a time when she should have been assisted by her two daughters-in-law, she had none by her side. Her dreams looked shattered. But she never expressed any harsh feelings against her sons and their wives. "Afterall, they have their families to look after," she reminded Badri Prasad, who very often talked of their sons' indifference.

A life without much activity after retirement had made Badri Prasad somewhat peevish. Once or twice he toyed with the idea of doing some part-time job, but Basanti Devi had refrained him. She was concerned with his hypertension condition.

Though younger in age, Varmaji and Krishnaswami, two of their neighbours and their families, had been providing a nice company to Badri Prasad and his wife ever since they shifted to their own ground floor flat after Badri Prasad's retirement. Basanti Devi had been acting as a guide and philosopher to the women.

Teaching them recipes, helping them in their knitting and stitching work, and rendering assistance in their other day-to-day chores gave Basanti a kind of pleasure that helped her forget the absence of her own daughters-in-law. But for the care and help of the neighbours, Badri Prasad and his wife would have been leading a miserable life.

But when alone in their flat they did get a feeling of loneliness. They yearned for some company. They wanted somebody to be around. Had their sons not chosen to be away from them, their flat would have been buzzing with activity. There would have been sounds of giggles, cries, shouts, laughters. But those on whom they had pinned their hopes had let them down.

For their elder son, Roshan, who had settled in London, they were as good as dead. Badri Prasad had drawn on all his financial resources to help him go abroad for higher studies. He did not want anything to stand in his son's way.

"I do not want you to feel that your father deprived you of an opportunity," he had told Roshan. "But my son, you must come back. Your mother will certainly miss you."

But instead of coming back Roshan married an English girl and decided to settle there. The news came as a big shock to Badri Prasad and Basanti Devi. For days they could not recover. But the time healed their wounds.

Roshan did make occasional visits to India. But these provided no consolation to Badri Prasad and his wife. The gifts he brought or sent through others were no substitute for the love and warmth their grandchildren would have given them.

"It is no good a place for the old people," Roshan had replied when Badri Prasad had once expressed his desire to settle in England. "Moreover, the language will be a big problem for

Mummy. Kitty and the kids do not understand a word of Hindi. However, in case you want to come here for a pleasure trip, you are welcome. But I may not be able to spare money for your trip immediately." Badri Prasad never wrote a word about the visit after that.

Raman, the younger son, on the other hand, had preferred Bombay to Delhi. He got employment in Bombay. He chose his wife, a colleague, from there. He even purchased an apartment in Bombay. Rather, he made his intentions clear that he would finally settle there only. All this naturally pained Badri Prasad.

Badri Prasad's requests to Raman to try for his transfer to Delhi were ignored. "Both your mummy and I want some company", he had pleaded with him in one of his letters. "Your wife and children will provide a very good company to us. There will be some life around us."

But Raman, without making any serious efforts for his and his wife's transfer, had expressed his inability in this regard. "It is difficult for Madhuri and me to get a simultaneous transfer," he had replied and added a rider to close the issue for all times to come. "As Madhuri has been brought up and educated in Bombay, she may find it difficult to adjust to a new situation in Delhi."

Even to Badri Prasad's suggestion that he would sell off his Delhi flat and shift to Bombay, Raman's response was not very encouraging. "I don't think you will be comfortable over here in case you decide to stay here permanently", he had written. After that Badri Prasad and Basanti never broached the idea further.

But it was the latest communication from Raman that had distressed Badri Prasad and his wife. It was in response to Badri Prasad's letter wherein he had informed his son that his mother was not keeping well and a change of climate and place would do a lot of good to her.

"Have you sent a reply to Raman's letter?" asked Basanti Devi as she got up to go to the kitchen.

"No, not yet," Badri Prasad replied. And, probably as an afterthought, added,. "What is there to reply? He wants us to postpone our visit to summer. We have no choice" There was a feeling of helplessness in his expression.

Basanti Devi looked at her husband in dismay.

"Why summer?" It seemed Badri Prasad had been brooding over the contents of Raman's letter. "Was it not January when he had come all the way to fetch you for the second delivery of his wife?" he queried in a tone full of anguish.

"You are unnecessarily trying to read too much in his letter," remarked Basanti Devi in order to pacify Badri Prasad. "May be he is genuinely concerned about our convenience."

"We are not going to Bombay, whether it is summer or winter," Badri Prasad said in a voice that sounded bitter. "And I am going to write the same to him."

"But we can ask him to come to Delhi along with his family for a short visit," suggested Basanti Devi. "We will have a nice time. We can curtail some of our expenses and save a part of your pension for their visit." She looked overjoyed. Probably a feeling of having every body around her was already being experienced by her.

"We are not going to do anything of the sort," Badri Prasad said in a somewhat harsh tone. "If the neighbours are going to look after us and are finally to cremate us, why should we be bothering about these good-for-nothing sons".

Badri Prasad's statement, though sour and bitter, indicated the reality they were facing. Basanti Devi did not dispute his statement.

The doorbell rang.

"I will go and see," said Basanti Devi. Ramesh, Varmaji's son, was there.

"Uncle, we are planning to go for a picnic. Daddy wants you and aunty to come with us. He has gone to arrange for a van."

"Oh, sure." Badri Prasad jumped with joy. Looking at his wife, he said, "Your aunty will prepare potato curry for everybody." Basanti gave a broad smile as she nodded in affirmative. For a moment, they forgot their sons, their families, and the letter.

*** *** ***

THE SECOND CUP

He sipped the coffee. She followed suit. There had been no exchange of words between them for the last few minutes.

At last he broke the silence and in his usual smooth tone said, "Now, listen Rajni, the decision has to be taken by you and you alone. I shall be the last person to impose myself on you."

There was no harshness, no bitterness, in his tone, despite their past days looming large on this meeting.

She did not say anything; did not even lift her eyes from her cup; fearing her eyes might betray her.

He had another sip and tapped his fingers on the saucer.

Again there was silence and again he broke it. "I could never imagine, Rajni, that you would make such an issue of that tiny tiff between us."

To call that wordy duel that had taken place between them just six months after their marriage and which had culminated in her departure for her parents house a tiny tiff showed his magnanimity.

Three months of separation had brought no change in him he was as calm and composed as she had observed him on the first day after her marriage.

Even before their marriage she had heard about his straight-forwardness; a man having no inhibitions at all. In fact her father, when he had suggested his name the first time had said, "Rajni, you are getting married to a man with whom you shall have to be straight-forward to make your marital life happy."

But she had often wondered how a man without any crookedness or inhibitions had risen to the post of a director in such a big firm.

But to-day, sitting across the coffee table, he was proving himself true. "Do you think I was wrong in telling you the truth.

Calling a spade a spade". He again weighed every word, and after a pause said, "I am very sure, Rajni, you too would have later on laughed over the whole matter."

She wanted to say, "No, I did not laugh over it. But gave a serious thought to what he had said and found how correct he was." But self-respect and self-ego, prohibited her from saying it. Had that been not the case, she would have certainly gone back to him by now. In fact this meeting too had been called by him. He had sent her a letter asking her to meet him. Even in that small and to the point letter he was very straight forward. "I do not want to meet you to lecture you about anything. But to know your mind; to feel if there has been any transformation in you by now. To be very frank, I must confess that the last three months of separation has confirmed my belief that we are made for each other, the belief which togetherness of six months could not confirm."

She could not say no to his request. She wanted to grab this opportunity of meeting him; facing him; confirming his belief. Now sitting before him on the coffee table, she cursed herself for taking such an irrational and drastic decision of leaving him. Little understanding on her part, would not have brought the matters to this crisis.

Sailing was smooth in their married life, till Suraj, an executive in Ranjan's company, arrived on the scene. Ranjan's busy and tight official schedule always kept him on his toes. If he was to attend the directors' meeting in the morning, he was to take a guest from abroad for luncheon in the afternoon. Dining out with somebody or the other was almost a daily affair. To top it all, touring the country over to supervise the work of the sale task force, kept him away from home for about 10 days in a month. Occasionally she also accompanied Ranjan on such tours but found them altogether choking. These dinners, dance parties, cocktails, were nothing but circus arenas where one had to tight walk on the rope of etiquette.

Ranjan was conscious about that : for once he confessed, "Rajni, I know you must be feeling bored at times with nobody to accompany you for movies and shopping. But darling, these modern management techniques require all this running about. The company bosses only want the results; they do not realise how strenuous it is and that too at the cost of one's family life."

Perhaps all that was weighing in his mind when one day he brought Suraj with him and introduced him to her.

But desperation had continued to grow in her. Perhaps these moods were responsible for seeking constant company of Suraj, who was introduced to her by Ranjan himself at one of the company's get-together. "Rajni, meet Suraj, an executive in my firm; a very enjoyable person. He is an all-rounder, having interest in almost everything under the sky. Movies, rummy, bridge, eating, talking and what not. In fact a good company for anybody."

Suraj really was a good company. Be it a new movie, a cabaret in a restaurant, rummy sessions in the card rooms of the clubs, he escorted her. The boredom in her life had almost vanished. His company had given her altogether a new taste of life. But she was unaware of the strains her relations with Ranjan were being put into. Not only she was neglecting the home, but Ranjan also. Whether it was bed time or breakfast or tiffins for his office lunch, she did everything half-heartedly. Ranjan had pointed this to her in his own way. "Rajni, it seems you require a refresher course in cooking. You have forgotten your pre-marriage lessons."

And instead of taking this in the spirit it was said, she had flared up and shouted, "What do you mean?"

Ranjan had simply smiled away the query. Rajni had again repeated, "What do you mean?"

"You know, Rajni, what I am pointing at. I need not explain. Sometimes explanations make confusion worse confounded."

It was Rajni who had started explaining. "I know you do not like my moving about; my friendship with Suraj. You cannot stand his attention towards me. But who is to be blamed? You, and you only. You never bothered about me. It was always your office and officialdom. You took me for granted for everything and thought that I would fit in any sort of hubs of the wheel. What you forgot was that even wheels start creaking without greasing."

"You are turning philosophic", Ranjan had said smilingly.

"Don't take it as a fun. I am serious", Rajni was emphatic.

"But Rajni, I would like you to see the things in right perspective. At the moment you are agitated."

Agitated she was, no doubt. In the same agitated frame of mind she had decided to leave Ranjan and his house.

They had again gone back to their shells.

"Did you meet Suraj any of these day?" He had touched upon a sensitive subject. She was not prepared for it. "Or should I put it: Did Suraj meet you?" There was just a flutter in her eyes. She had no answer to this question. The fact was that Suraj never bothered to meet her after she had left Ranjan. Ranjan gauged her embarrassment. "I know he would not have. For it was you who sought his company. He had many to give him. Rajni, I would not have felt your moving with him but for the way he exploited this for his personal ends. He publicised to everybody the way you treated him .....", he paused and searched for words, "the way your relations went with him.... He almost blackmailed me....." Rajni just listened. But she admired his courage to speak to her without any rancour.

Ranjan ordered another coffee. "I know you don't like a second cup of coffee."

How sweet of him to continue to care for her likes and dislikes, she thought.

"But ..... Ranjan ......", she was hesitant, "these three months have brought a change in me. I shall love to have a second cup". And the tears rolled down her eyes.

*** *** ***

DEATH TO VIKRAM

I had a sigh of relief when I was told about Vikram's death. Man like him did not deserve to be on this earth, I thought.

He did not suffer from any dreadful disease. He was admitted in the hospital with a complaint of abdominal pain, which was later diagnosed as ulcers. A restless person like Vikram was bound to get ulcers, I had imagined.

I was sure the hospital staff would have also heaved a sigh of relief. The doctor in-charge of his ward had complained to me. "Your friend has become a headache for all of us. Why should he bother about others?" I wanted to tell the doctor that Vikram was born to bother about others.

I smiled.

The doctor had complained that Vikram had provoked other wardmates and had asked them not to accept the sub-standard food supplied by hospital authorities. "After all the government spends so much on these hospitals," he had told them. He had accused the doctors and other hospital staff of making money even at the cost of the miseries of other people.

I had told Vikram not to interfere in the working of the hospital. The doctors and the other staff did not like it and he was prejudicing them.

For the first time he had listened to me without any argument. He had wept. He was a broken man. A man who, possibly, had no more interest in anything. He had said, "You will not hear any more complaints about me." After a pause he had further said, "I should die now."

It seemed as if he was responding to everybody's call of death to Vikram.

Vikram had been a fighter since the day I had known him.

A fighter for the causes. He would not swallow anything and everything. He had suffered for his convictions.

His father once had asked him to leave home. Vikram had reported to the police that his father, mother and brother were torturing his sister-in-law (brother's wife) and wanted to kill her because she did not bring enough dowry. Vikram was accused of having illicit relations with her and kicked out from the house. After a few days he heard that she had committed suicide.

No one from Vikram's family bothered for him after that.

His own marriage was a peculiar affair. "I would like to marry a destitute girl from a rescue home", he had announced one day.

He had wanted me to arrange it because no one from his family was any more interested in his affairs. But even the marriage had proved disastrous for him. "It is becoming increasingly impossible to pull on with Sunita". He had informed me within six months of his marriage.

"Why? What happened ?"

"She feels that I am not earning sufficient to lead a comfortable life. Her life with me is probably worse than what she had led at Nari Niketan". And without any contempt and rancour he continued, "I do not blame her at all. Any person in her position would have felt the same way. If the life continues to be hell for her, what does it matter whether she is with me or at Nari Niketan."

A few days later, he had sent Sunita back to the rescue home. "I shall bring her back as and when I am in a position to provide her with a life she deserves"

Job-wise Vikram had been a rolling stone. He had started his career with a secured job of a clerk in a government office; but left it after a year. "Nobody wants to work in a government office and one who wants to work is ridiculed. I can't be dishonest to myself", he used to argue.

He had joined another office; an undertaking doing building construction work on behalf of the government. He resigned within a month.

"You know", he had told me, "in that office everything moved on the wheels of corruption. I could not be a party to that".

I had felt sorry for him. He was trying to search gold from the earth which perhaps was not suited even for the potter.

His uncompromising attitude had brought many troubles to him. He was again without a job.

Through an influence I had got him a job in a private firm. There too he got restless and expressed his desire to resign. Vikram could not stay there long.

At long last he had settled in a saleman's job in a company manufacturing some consumer products. He had found it very satisfying. "This job is like rowing your own boat without anybody else in it. You are always honest to your products without condemning the others."

I could not understand Vikram's logic. He might have liked the rules of a saleman's profession, where he was not asked to compromise with his principles.

That the death should have come to him at a time when he was settling down in his life was perhaps God's wish.

No one from his family bothered to claim his body from the hospital. Sunita did come; not to claim the body, but assets he might have left. Vikram had left none. Along with his body the hospital people handed over a note addressed to me.

"Do not perform any rites for me. I do not deserve any".

*** *** ***

JOURNEY ENDS

There had been no change in the train's speed for the last one hour. Manoj checked the time on his watch. Still three hours to go. During the last 12 hours he had gone through all the reading material he had got at Bombay VT. Most of the time he had been alone in the compartment : some passengers boarding and getting down at some wayside stations after one or two hours' journey. He had slept through the night's journey. It was the day's travelling that was taxing him. He was anxious to reach his destination, his village.

He was returning home after three years of stay in USA. As a matter of fact, he had promised his parents that immediately on completion of his studies over there he would come back to the village, not only to use the new techniques in agriculture for himself but to teach the same to village folk also. Instead, he got a job in Bombay and was there for the last six months. He had not even informed his parents about his arrival in India.

From USA too, Manoj had barely sent half-a-dozen letters to his Bapu. On not getting regular replies to his letters, his Bapu had stopped writing to him. A communication gap had developed between the father and son — his Bapu almost writing off his only son. Whenever Manoj's mother chided her husband for not writing to Manoj he would say : "Forget about that good for nothing fellow. Think that we had no child. My only regret is that I spent so much on him to find him to be of no use either to us or to this village".

Though Banwari Lal was a zamindar having the largest holding, he had a reputation of treating all with respect and love. He never berated anybody. Even the labour who worked on his land was shown all the regard and not looked down with spite.

"They are the real bread earners for us." He used to tell everybody. "But for them we are nowhere." He had told the same to Manoj. "Never be a boss to them. Be a friend."

The advice was repeated again by Banwari Lal before Manoj had left for America. "I will not like you to be a pig-headed person after your return from abroad. The land and the labour are our backbone. Be grounded in the culture of this country, my son."

But immediately on joining the university at America, Manoj had fallen for Kitty's beauty. Kitty's love had overtaken everything else including his village, parents, and Kamani; a simple, innocent, raw belle, daughter of a small farmer of his village.

Kamani, like many other women of the village, was very often seen in Banwari Lal's house. She had lost her mother when she was hardly one. In Manoj's mother she had found the love and affection which God had denied her.

Manoj was attracted towards Kamani first time when he was leaving his village to join a town college for his graduation.

In her innocent way she had asked him, "Will you forget me?"

"Why this question, Kammo?"

"I would like you to be always with me."

They had grown together. It was only now that they were parting. And that parting had developed a feeling in them which could be termed love.

Every visit to the village brought Manoj closer to Kamani. But his decision to go to USA for higher studies came as a bombshell for her.

"Why do you want to go there, Manu?"

"But I shall be coming back to village."

"You would not be visiting the village every week."

"No..... But when I come back, first thing I do is to marry my Kammo."

"Are you sure ?", Kamani had asked Manoj in a matter-of-factly tone. Manoj had simply laughed away Kamani's query.

"But .... Manu .... you shall never find a girl like me," she had prophesied and her prophesy had come true.

While proposing to Kitty, Manoj had told her that they would have to go back to India and settle there. Kitty had accepted the proposal but did not agree to the suggestion that they should go back to India after marriage.

"But I have my aged parents over there. And moreover Kitty I would like to go back to my country."

"That means you love your parents and country more than me." Kitty had given an abrupt reply.

She jilted Manoj and by the end of the academic session she married an American boy, a few years younger to her in age. Shocked and dejected Manoj decided to go back to India. He applied for a job and accepted an offer made by a big Bombay firm.

Manoj's work in Bombay kept him so busy that he could not find any time to go to his village. He was fighting shy of sending a letter to his parents.

Rita, his secretary, was his constant companion in Bombay : a companionship very badly needed by Manoj.

But success in love was perhaps not Manoj's cup of life. John Arthur, a British expert, who had joined Manoj's firm as consultant, showed undue interest in Rita and got her transferred as his personal assistant. Rita got so much enamoured of her new boss that whenever she met Manoj she had nothing else to talk but Arthur.

"The guy is smart". She had once told Manoj almost teasing him. "It is really rewarding to spend evenings with him. He talks of everything : movies, politics, ... and love. He has almost .... fallen in love ..... with our country ..... and me". She had told Manoj without a blush. And within a week Arthur and Rita had announced their engagement.

The news had come as a big shock for Manoj. He resigned his job and decided to go back to his village.

The train had slowed down. Manoj checked the time. An hour's journey was still there. He was getting restless.

"Will his parents, other village folks .... and Kammo show the same love and affection for him?" Doubts started creeping in his mind.

The train had again slowed down. He could smell his village. The surroundings looked familiar.

The train halted with a jerk. As he stepped out of the compartment he heard shouts of Rahman, a tongawalla from his village. ''Is there somebody going to the village?''

''Rahman Chacha!'' Manoj bent down to touch his feet.

''Are you not Pandit's son?''

Manoj replied in the affirmative.

''What a coincidence? You are in time for ...''

''For what ?'' anxious Manoj interrupted. ''For Kammo's marriage. Your Bapu is performing it. Pandit is really a great man doing everything for this orphan girl.'' And Rahman hit hard the horse with the whip. Manoj shivered as Rahman further lashed at the horse.

*** *** ***